The Unicorn and the Lost Cat

Written by Claire Philip   Illustrated by Jessica Rose

Miles Kelly

It was a beautiful spring evening, and Elsie was about to go to bed.

"Where's Charlie?" she asked her Dad. "I can't go to sleep without my cat!"

They searched for him in all the usual places, yet Charlie was nowhere to be seen.

"He'll come home when he's hungry," said Dad.

Elsie was worried. Charlie never stayed out at night.

She tried to sleep, but moonlight was shining in through the window and keeping her awake.

Elsie went to close the curtains and saw a **sleeping animal** under the tree in her garden.

"Is that a deer... wait, no, it's a UNICORN!"

Elsie crept downstairs and into the garden. She tiptoed over to the sleeping creature.

It heard her coming, and woke up!

"Hello Elsie, I've come to help you find Charlie," said the unicorn.

This made Elsie cry. When the unicorn saw this, it nuzzled her shoulder.

Elsie placed her hand on the unicorn and asked, "Is this all real?"

"Yes, my name is Comet. I am a real unicorn."

"Wow!" said Elsie.

"Do you know where my cat is?" she asked.
Comet closed his eyes, then said...

"I can see he's trapped inside a
greenhouse not far away!"

"Please will you help me rescue him?" cried Elsie.

"Of course!" said the unicorn. "Climb onto my back."

When she was sat comfortably, Elsie whispered, "Charlie, we're coming to get you!"

Comet rose up into the air.

Elsie was so excited!

They flew up above the village and soared over the nearby valley.

Very soon Comet began heading back down to the ground.

They landed softly in a beautiful
garden, next to a greenhouse.

Inside were all kinds of
fruits and vegetables.

Elsie spotted Charlie at the window.

"Charlie I'm here! And you'll never guess what... I flew on a UNICORN!"

Comet gently
tapped his spiral horn
against the glass.

It disappeared
straight away!

"Charlie!" called Elsie, and the cat ran out and jumped into her arms.

Purr purr!

"Let's go home!" said Elsie.

She climbed onto Comet's back once more, and Charlie jumped up next to her.

"Home sweet home!" called Elsie, as they landed back in her garden.

"Thank you so much Comet!"

They were all very tired,
so they lay down.

Cuddled up together, all three fell fast asleep.

Before long, the birds started to sing and the sun began to rise. It was time to say goodbye to Comet. Elsie hugged her new unicorn friend.

"It's morning," she said. "We'd better go back inside!"

"Come back soon Comet!" said Elsie, "and thank you again!"

Elsie had just sat down in the kitchen when her Dad walked in. He saw Charlie and said...

"I told you he'd come home when he was hungry!"